DODO EVERY DAY

DODO EVERY DAY

Story and Pictures by

ILSE-MARGRET VOGEL

Harper & Row, Publishers
New York, Hagerstown, San Francisco, London

DODO EVERY DAY
Copyright © 1977 by Ilse-Margret Vogel

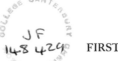

FIRST EDITION

Library of Congress Cataloging in Publication Data
Vogel, Ilse-Margret.
  Dodo every day.

  SUMMARY: A little girl tells about her relationship with her grandmother.
  [1. Grandmothers–Fiction]   I. Title.
PZ7.V867Do   [E]   76-24302
ISBN 0-06-026315-6
ISBN 0-06-026316-4 lib. bdg.

I called her Dodo.

She was my grandmother and I loved her very much. The name Dodo was the result of many tries to say grandmother when I was little.

I loved her then. I loved her when I grew up. I loved her after she died. And I love her now.

This book is for her.

CONTENTS

I AM SAD

I could tell Dodo everything. "Today I am sad," I said, leaning my head against her shoulder.

"Why are you sad?" she asked.

"I don't know," I admitted, "but just the same I am sad. Very sad."

We were in the kitchen. Dodo was peeling apples. We were alone except for Velvet Paw, the cat, who was sleeping next to the stove.

"You have a nice apple pie to look forward to," Dodo said cheerfully.

"I am too sad for apple pie," I whispered, trying to fight back my tears.

"All right. Be sad for a little while," Dodo said. She put one arm around me and, in this awkward position, went on peeling apples.

I watched Dodo's skillful hands peel off the pretty red skin. The fruity smell of the white inner flesh got stronger as the apple became more naked. The smell was good, and Dodo's arm around my neck seemed a wall against my sadness. I felt content.

Then Dodo began to sing a little song. The one I liked so much. It told about a bird in an elderberry bush. It was the middle of May, the elderberry bush was in full bloom, and the little bird sang a song of longing and love and faith. The bird was sad because a little girl that used to come and sit under the bush every day had not come for a long time. But the bird's song was so urgent and so strong that the girl *did* show up in the end, and everything was fine.

I began to feel good again. I was happy to be close to Dodo, Dodo who was suddenly everything. She was the bird and she was the song. She was the blooming elderberry bush that gave shelter to bird and song. And the girl that returned to the bush? Was it I? I would think about it at night in bed, and if I wasn't sure, I would ask Dodo in the morning.

After Dodo had finished the song, she removed her arm from my shoulder, picked up an extra large apple and said, "Now watch. Watch closely. This apple is very special and it is for you."

She held the large red-cheeked apple in her left hand and began to peel it. She began at the stem. Slowly, very slowly, she guided the small paring knife in circles around the apple without breaking the band of skin. Longer and longer grew the band, forming a spiral as it hung down. Dodo had to raise both hands so the long peel would not touch her lap. I held my breath. Even Velvet Paw woke up and watched. The band of apple skin was so thin it was transparent. Like a magician, Dodo swayed and weaved, back and forth, and brought

her knife to the smallest circle around the blossom part of the apple. Then the peel came off. I had held my breath the last few seconds, but now I broke into laughter of relief.

"This is your apple and this is your apple chain," Dodo said, giving me both.

We laughed and were happy.

I AM BORED

"Are you sad again?" asked Dodo, when I entered her room. She put her hand under my chin, raised my head and, as always, looked straight into my eyes.

"No, today I am not sad," I answered. "Today I am bored."

"Bored?" Dodo asked. "What is that?"

"Oh, Dodo, you know," I said. "You know what it means to be bored."

"No, dear, I do not know," insisted Dodo. "Can you explain?"

I had to think awhile. "Well," I said, "it is . . . it feels . . . all hollow inside. I am not sad and I am not glad. I'm not anything at all. It's worse than being sad."

"Oh, my," Dodo said, "that does not sound so good. Has it happened to you before, my poor darling?"

I nodded.

"There are so many wonderful things to do," Dodo said. "Have you . . . ?"

"I have done them all," I interrupted. "ALL! I have dressed and undressed my doll Lisa a hundred times. I have given her all the hairdos I can think of. I even started to read my favorite book again, but it's boring. I know it by heart."

"Oh, my," Dodo said again, shaking her head.

"It's still an hour till suppertime," I went on,

"and I don't even know what to do for the next five minutes. I'm so bored."

"Come over here to the table," Dodo said. "You always like to look at things on my table."

This was true. The table in my grandmother's room was like no other table I had ever seen. It looked like a dining table, but it was not empty as dining tables usually are. It held many wonderful things—a flowerpot with a begonia that seemed to bloom forever. A tall silver candlestick with a wax candle that smelled like honey when it was lit. A tiny cup inlaid with green, blue, and yellow enamel pieces and filled with toothpicks. A brass cat, not much taller than my thumb, that came from India. And, best of all, a bell in the shape of a lady. When you lifted her by her head, the tongue would swing against the inside of her brass skirt and make a clear, lovely and surprisingly loud sound. And then still more flowers, wild flowers or flowers of the season, in old copper mugs or in pretty blue and amber bottles. When the sunlight hit these bottles, they cast blue and amber streaks of light all over the tabletop.

But now there was no sunlight, and I felt numb and joyless.

"Sit down at the table," Dodo said, "and we will play a game."

We both sat down. Dodo told me to put my face on the table, and I did.

"No, no, not the chin," she said. "Put your cheek down and close both your eyes."

I did as Dodo said but wondered what good could come of that.

"When I ring the lady-bell, you will open one eye," Dodo said. "One eye only."

At the sound of the bell, I opened one eye. Dodo, too, had put her face on the tabletop, and for a second we looked eye to eye.

"Now think little," Dodo said. "Don't raise your head! Think *little*. Think worm. A *tiny* worm. Think bug. A *tiny* bug."

"Ladybug," I said.

"All right, ladybug," Dodo said. "Shiny red wings, black little dots. You have five black dots and I have seven." She paused, then began to sing softly.

13

Ladybug, ladybug, don't fly away
Ladybug, ladybug, I want you to stay
Ladybug, ladybug, go find your way. . . .

And while she sang, I, ladybug, wandered all
over the tabletop. The begonia plant loomed over
me like a huge oak tree. The candlestick became a
tower so high that if I climbed it, I thought, I could
surely reach the sky. The brass cat looked taller
than the Egyptian Sphinx I had seen in a travel
book. The bell-lady was larger than the huge statue
in the town square. The wild flowers in mugs and
bottles bent over and touched the ground I was
walking on. Their sweetness made me take a deep
breath and close my tired eye.

I felt Dodo's hand on my head and heard the
bell ring again. Then Dodo's cheerful voice
announced, "It's close to suppertime. Let's go downstairs and you can help mother."

I shook my head, stood up and looked down at
the table. It looked as it always looked. It had lost
its magic, though not its beauty. And yet I knew
I could come back anytime and take another walk

among the towering trees and tall statues. I touched the little bell and looked up at Dodo. She opened the door. The smell of potato pancakes, hot applesauce and syrup came up from the kitchen. Hand in hand we walked downstairs.

I AM JEALOUS

"Dodo, what is Mozart?" I asked.

Dodo put down her sewing and looked at me. " 'Who is Mozart?' you should ask. But why do you ask? And what do you know about Mozart?"

"Nothing," I answered. "But I hate Mozart."

Dodo gave me a long, puzzled look. "How can you hate somebody you do not even know?" she asked.

17

"Because," I said, "because . . . I am jealous."

"Jealous of Mozart?" she asked in disbelief.

I nodded. "You see, Uncle Karl doesn't like me anymore. All he cares about is Mozart."

"I can't believe that," Dodo said.

"But it's true, Dodo, it is."

"Well—tell me."

"You see, I wanted to show Uncle Karl a picture I had made. A really good picture of Velvet Paw. Uncle Karl was in the living room reading a book. When I started to talk to him, he just hushed me up and without even looking at me said, 'Later.' I sat down next to him and waited. I waited a long time, but later never came. Uncle Karl turned page after page. He smiled. He looked happy. He didn't seem to know I was there. And the book didn't even have any pictures. There was just one word on the cover in big black letters. It said *Mozart*." I stopped.

Was Dodo still listening to me? She walked over to the shelf next to her bed and pulled out a folder. She opened the folder and leafed through pages of loose sheets with faces—faces with beards, faces

surrounded by mountains of curls, faces peeking out of high stiff collars and faces with cascades of lace under their chins.

Finally she pulled out one sheet and announced, "Here is Mozart!"

I looked. "Oh, she is pretty," I murmured.

Dodo laughed. "*He* is pretty. It is young Mozart when he was twelve years old."

I took a closer look. Curls fell over the narrow high forehead. A tail of hair bound in a ribbon was at the back of the head. There were delicate ruffles of lace from the chin down the shirtfront. He was sitting at a piano.

"They dressed like that over a hundred years ago," Dodo explained and took out a second picture. "This is Mozart when he was older." There were still ruffles and curls; the nose was somewhat larger and sharper now, but the face was still very pretty.

I kept looking at the two faces.

"He was a composer," Dodo said. "He wrote and played very fine music. His life was full of excitement and work. He traveled through many

20

countries, playing his music for kings and queens, and everybody loved him." She paused, then asked, "Can you understand, now, that Uncle Karl is eager to know about him? When you wanted to show the picture of Velvet Paw to Uncle Karl, he might have been in the middle of a wonderful concert. Books can do that, you know. They can take you to places and into events."

"They can?" I asked.

"Yes, the right words can have great power. And if Uncle Karl was carried away by them, it does not mean he does not love you anymore. You needn't be jealous of a book."

"I'll go and ask Uncle Karl," I said.

"Wait," said Dodo, "I know something better." She took a chair to the high shelf in the corner, climbed on it and rummaged through all kinds of things. When she stepped down, she put a little box in front of me. On top of the box was a picture of a girl in a swing, surrounded by a garland of roses. On one side was a small crank for turning.

"Wind it," Dodo said. "Wind it slowly and

carefully so you will not overwind and break it."

When I finished winding and let go, clear silvery music filled the room. It sounded so happy it made me want to dance.

"This is a minuet by Mozart," Dodo whispered. Her head shook with the rhythm of the music, and her gray curls danced over her forehead.

When the music stopped, I wound the box again. This time Dodo took my hands, and together we danced what she called a "little minuet." When we stopped, she was breathless.

"May I take the music box down to show Uncle Karl?" I asked.

"Yes, you may," Dodo said, "but make sure you don't disturb him."

I hurried downstairs. Uncle Karl was in the same spot with the book in his hands. I tiptoed to the sofa, sat down beside him and wound the music box. After the first few notes he put the book down, smiled at me and listened.

"Thank you," he said, "thank you. That was just what I needed. I have finished the book and am a

little sad. It's like saying good-bye to a dear friend."
He reached for my hand, squeezed it and said, "But
now I have you to tell about Mozart."

"Yes, please do," I answered. "I love Mozart."

I AM ASHAMED

Dodo found me huddled in the bushes at the end of our large garden. She had called a couple of times, but I had not answered. I could not face her. I felt too guilty and ashamed. But Dodo must have known about this secret hiding spot, because she came walking straight toward me.

The branches of the forsythia bush touched the ground on all sides. Once I had penetrated the thick

26

curtain of twigs and leaves, which always pull my hair and dress, I sat down comfortably as if inside a tent.

Dodo parted the branches with her hands and said, "There you are. Why didn't you answer me?"

I had not answered for fear Dodo would hear the tears in my voice.

"Come out," she said. "I want to talk to you."

And still I couldn't answer.

"Well, if you won't come out," said Dodo, "I will have to come in." The branches cracked and bent and, hunched over, Dodo struggled in. I buried my face in my arms. I did not want her to see my red eyes. When she sat down and put her arm around me, I turned away.

"You would not want to sit beside me if you knew," I sobbed.

"Knew what?" she asked.

"If you knew what I did to Velvet Paw."

"I know you love Velvet Paw," Dodo said, "and you are always kind to her."

"I don't love her anymore, and I was not kind to her."

"That is hard to believe," Dodo said.

"But it's true," I said, "it really is. I threw a big rock at her, it hit her and she limped off into the bushes."

"I have never seen you throw a stone at anything," Dodo said. "Why did you do that?"

"Because I felt like it," I answered.

"But why?" Dodo asked.

How could I begin to tell? I did not know what I felt. I felt anger and love, pity and hatred, shame and guilt all at the same time.

"Tell me what happened," Dodo said.

"You will not love me anymore if I tell you," I answered.

"I will always love you," said Dodo. "I might be unhappy if you do something wrong, but I could not stop loving you."

"I don't want to make you unhappy, Dodo."

"We will bear it together," she said.

"Well, you see," I stammered, "you see . . . I love Velvet Paw so much. But when I saw this little mouse in her paws, bleeding, I loved the little mouse too. And then it happened so fast. The rock was

near my foot, I picked it up and threw it at Velvet Paw; she gave a scream and limped away. But the little mouse was dead." After a pause, I asked, "Do you still love me, Dodo?"

"Of course I do," Dodo said. "And I still love Velvet Paw, too. And the little mouse." We sat in silence.

"Come now, we will go to the house," Dodo said. We struggled out through the dense branch curtain. When we reached the porch, Velvet Paw was sitting on the railing, washing her left paw. She saw me, stopped washing and came limping toward me to rub against my legs. I started to cry again. Dodo picked her up, put her in my arms and said, "You see, Velvet Paw has forgiven you. Why can't you forgive yourself?"

I AM PROUD

The rain had stopped. I had watched the short spring shower from my window. Now I ran out to the garden. On the far end was one long vegetable bed. Mother had given it to me. "This is yours," she had said. "You can grow whatever you want."

Weeks ago, in early spring, I had sown radish seeds in one small part of the long strip of dirt. For weeks, while nothing happened, I had watered it and watched impatiently. Finally tiny green sprouts broke through the dark soil. And after a few days of warm sunshine, they grew fast.

As I approached the garden, a strong smell came to me from the rows of turned over, moist earth. It was delicious, a smell I had not known before. I took a deep breath. Then I looked at my radish patch, and where the green stems of the leaves touched the ground, I saw a faint touch of red.

I bent down, and with one finger I felt the swelling just below the surface of the soil. "A baby radish!" I exclaimed, and ran to the house to fetch Dodo.

She stopped her sewing, followed me to the garden and bent down to feel my baby radish. Just then, a little snake appeared from nowhere and slithered soundlessly past Dodo's fingers. It was a pretty little garter snake, I thought, but to my surprise Dodo screamed. She screamed and started to run.

I had never heard her scream before, nor had I seen her run so fast. I followed her to the back

porch, where she collapsed in a chair. She was out of breath. Her hands lay trembling in her lap.

"Dodo," I said, "Dodo, it's only a little garden snake. It doesn't do any harm. I have seen it often."

Dodo looked at me out of the corner of her eye but did not say a word.

"Wait," I said, and ran to my room for a book. I opened it to the chapter on snakes and tried to show Dodo a picture of a garden snake, but she turned away. The snake in the picture was very pretty. Two long yellow stripes went zigzagging along the full length of its body.

"Listen, Dodo, listen," I pleaded, and I began to read: " 'Garter snakes, often called garden snakes, are not poisonous. They are useful animals since they feed partly on rats, insects and other pests. Because some people have mistaken ideas about them, they want to destroy these harmless snakes.' " I stopped and looked in Dodo's face.

"Let me see," she said, and took the book from my hand. For a long time she looked at the picture. "Yes," she said, "that is the same kind of snake that nearly bit my finger."

"They do not bite fingers," I told her as Dodo went on reading about the garden snake. I stood quietly beside her, stroking her hand.

After a while she put down the book and said, "All right. I will not be afraid of garden snakes anymore."

My heart began to beat fast with pride. I held on to her hand and said, "Dodo, whenever you are afraid of anything, you can turn to me."

"I will, my darling. I certainly will," said Dodo. Her face was all sun and smiles again, and I was proud. So proud.

I AM HAPPY

"Tomorrow is New Year's Eve," Dodo said to me. "Do you remember?"

"No," I answered, and with a meaningful smile I added, "I remember something else."

"What could that be?" asked Dodo, trying to match my smile.

"Wait and see," I said.

December thirty-first was Dodo's birthday. It

was a very nice and special day for me, nearly as good as my own birthday—not only because I always got what Dodo called a no-birthday present from her, but also because there was something to look forward to after Christmas. How sorry I felt for Hanna, the girl next door, who was always sad a few days after Christmas. "It takes eight months till my birthday comes around," she moaned, "and a full year till Christmas!"

But I was lucky! I hardly had time to read all my Christmas books and make good use of all my other Christmas presents, when I had to think up a birthday gift for Dodo.

On New Year's Eve, the Christmas tree was still up in the Christmas room. We met in front of it before breakfast, to congratulate Dodo and give her her birthday presents, which were under the tree.

Dodo looked at the book, the lacy scarf and the warm slippers mother and father had put there for her, and smiled.

Then she looked at my present. I had made a picture for her. I had drawn a bush with very big, flat, white flowers on it. I knew the flowers were too big. But big flowers are like big love, I thought. And that was what I felt for Dodo. The bird also was too big. Now looking at it while Dodo held it in her hand, I suddenly felt ashamed. The picture was not good enough for her, I thought. But when I looked up and saw her happy smile, I was reassured. She thanked me with hugs and kisses, then bent down and picked up a wrapped square package.

"Here is your no-birthday present," she said. "Unwrap it." It was a music box. I could see it was not the one with the Mozart minuet, because on top of the box was a bird instead of a girl in a swing. I very much wanted to listen to its melody, but I wanted to do it when I was alone.

My parents were surprised when I said, "I'll wait till after breakfast to play it." But Dodo nodded. She understood.

After breakfast I went back into the Christmas room. For a long time I looked at the pretty picture of a bird on top of the box. Then I turned the handle carefully and slowly as Dodo had taught me.

The melody of the elderberry bush blooming in May, with the lonely little bird singing his song of longing and love and faith, filled the room.

I sat down under the Christmas tree, smelling its pine needles, and listened to the song of spring, remembering its flowers and its smells. I thought of winters and summers, of Christmases and birthdays, the big beautiful world. Christmas was over, but I was happy just the same. Poor Hanna, I thought. She will be unhappy now because she has to wait so long for her birthday. But I was lucky. I did not have to wait for special days. I had Dodo. I had Dodo every day.